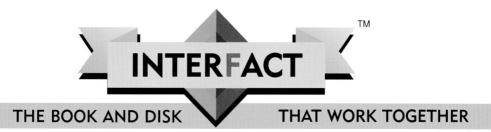

INTERFACT™

THE BOOK AND DISK   THAT WORK TOGETHER

DESERTS

PRINCETON ■ LONDON

Book and disk by
act-two Ltd

Published in the United States and Canada by
Two-Can Publishing LLC
234 Nassau Street
Princeton, NJ 08542

For information on other Two-Can books and multimedia,
Call 1-609-921-6700, fax 1-609-921-3349, or visit our web site at
http://www.two-canpublishing.com

ISBN: 1-58728-457-X

2 4 6 8 10 9 7 5 3 1

Photographic Credits: Front cover Bruce Coleman
Ardea: p14 tr, p21, p24; Bruce Coleman: p9, pp20-21, p22, p26 b;
Robert Harding: p18 b, p27; Hutchinson: p23; Frank Lane: pp10-11, p12 t;
Planet Earth Pictures: p13; Survival Anglia: p12 b, p18 t, p19;
Sygma: p26 tr; Zefa: pp14-15, pp16-17

Printed in Hong Kong by Wing King Tong

INTERFACT

THE BOOK AND DISK THAT WORK TOGETHER

INTERFACT will have you hooked in minutes—
and that's a fact!

The **CD-ROM is packed with
interactive activities, puzzles, quizzes,
and games that are
fun to do and full of
interesting facts.**

Meet some desert
animals and explore
their habitat with your
mouse.

Drag the
animals
into place
with your
mouse.

**Open the
book and discover
more fascinating
information
highlighted with
lots of full-color
illustrations and
photographs.**

Find out how
wind and rain
can change
the desert
landscape
over time.

To get the most out of **INTERFACT,**
use the book and CD-ROM together.
Look for the special signs called
Disk Links and Bookmarks. To find
out more, turn to page 40.

23

BOOKMARK

DISK LINK
See if you
can lead
the camels
to the oasis
in LOST FOR WORDS.

Once you've launched
INTERFACT, you'll never
look back.

LOAD UP!
Go to **page 38** to find out how to load
your disk and click into action.

HELP SCREEN

Learn how to use the disk in no time at all.

These are the controls the help screen will tell you how to use:
- arrow keys
- text boxes
- "hot" words

WHERE IN THE WORLD?

Explore the world's deserts with your mouse.

See the world's major deserts on screen and try labeling all of them. Then take a close up look at each one and find out all about life in that part of the world.

DESERTED!

Put your survival skills to the test in this interactive adventure game.

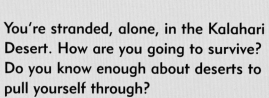

You're stranded, alone, in the Kalahari Desert. How are you going to survive? Do you know enough about deserts to pull yourself through?

KEEPING COOL

Meet Leo the Lizard and Sam the Snake—

the coolest reptiles around!

Sam the Snake has lots of questions about deserts—just like you! Luckily, Leo the Lizard is in the know. Click on him for all the answers.

4

How much rain falls in the Sahara every year?
- About ½ inch (1 cm)
- About 9 inches (10 cm)
- About 40 inches (100 cm)

BREAK THE DROUGHT

Use your desert know-how to stop the lake from drying out.

It hasn't rained around here for a very long time. Can you save the day? If you answer the quiz questions correctly, rain will fall. But if you get them wrong, the drought will only get worse.

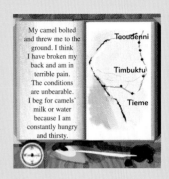

My camel bolted and threw me to the ground. I think I have broken my back and am in terrible pain. The conditions are unbearable. I beg for camels' milk or water because I am constantly hungry and thirsty.

Taoudenni
Timbuktu
Tieme

TREK TO TIMBUKTU

Get to know Renè Cailliè— a famous desert explorer.

Follow Cailliè's every footstep on his historical journey through the Sahara. Come back from time to time to read his journal and find out how he's been getting along.

DINNER TIME

Visit the desert creatures just in time for their evening meal.

Find out what's on the menu for the desert animals by completing the food web. Then explore the desert scene to learn about the plant and animal life.

O _ S _ S

LOST FOR WORDS

Can you point the camel caravan in the right direction?

These thirsty camels are going to an oasis. There's only one problem—they keep getting lost! Do you know enough desert words to help them on their way?

What's in the book

*All words in the text that appear in **bold** can be found in the glossary*

What are deserts?

Deserts are dry, barren places where there is very little rain. Deserts generally receive less than 10 inches (25 cm) of rain or snow each year. They also have particular types of soil and **vegetation**.

Many of the world's deserts are in hot areas, where the temperature often soars above 86 °F (30 °C). But some deserts, such as the Gobi Desert in Asia, are extremely cold. In winter, the temperature there can drop to 10 °F (-12 °C).

The areas around the North and South poles are also classified as deserts, and they are certainly cold!

Sand covers about 10 percent of desert areas. Other desert landscapes also have gravel, rocks, and mountains, or, in the polar regions, ice.

▶ These sand dunes are in the Namib Desert of southwestern Africa.

▼ A map of the world's major deserts

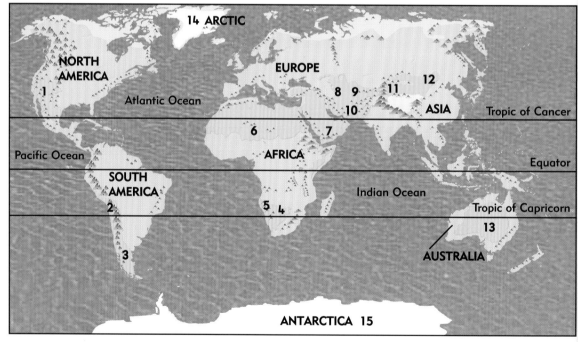

1. The North American deserts: the Great Basin, the Sonoran, Mojave, and Chihuahuan deserts, and Death Valley.
2. Atacama Desert
3. Patagonian Desert
4. Kalahari Desert
5. Namib Desert
6. Sahara
7. Arabian Desert
8. Kyzyl Kum
9. Karakum
10. Thar Desert
11. Taklimakan Desert
12. Gobi Desert
13. Australian Desert
14. Arctic
15. Antarctica

How do deserts form?

Many of the world's deserts lie directly north and south of the equator, in areas known as the tropics. Deserts in this area, such as the Sahara in Africa, are called tropical deserts. They are formed because of the movement of the air. At the equator, the air is very warm. It starts to rise and, as it does so, the air cools and releases its moisture as rain. This dry air moves away from the equator, toward the tropics. By the time it reaches the areas where the deserts lie, it has started to move back down toward the land and warm up again. This warm, dry air helps to create the desert **environment**.

DID YOU KNOW?

● The only regular supply of moisture to the Namib Desert in Africa is the fog that rolls in from the Atlantic Ocean every day.

DISK LINK
Do you want to know more about how deserts develop? Then ask a few questions in KEEPING COOL.

How a rain shadow desert is formed

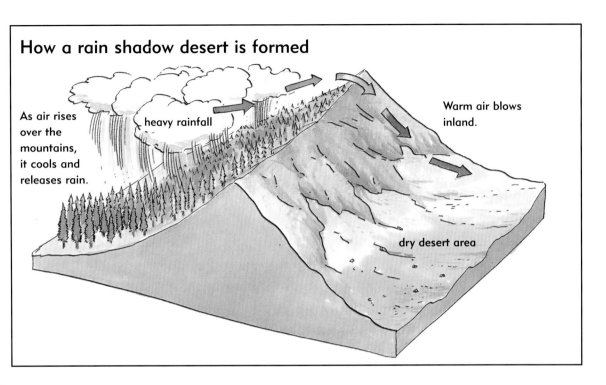

As air rises over the mountains, it cools and releases rain.

heavy rainfall

Warm air blows inland.

dry desert area

Some deserts, such as the Taklimakan Desert in China, lie in areas that are separated from the sea by mountains. Here, a rain shadow desert is created.

Coastal deserts, such as the Namib Desert in southwestern Africa, lie near the ocean. There, the air that moves across the ocean is cold and doesn't carry much moisture to the land.

Other deserts, such as the Gibson Desert in Australia, are far inland, where the air is dry.

◀ When it rains in the desert, the water may collect in channels or dry lake beds. Heavy, sudden downpours called **flash floods** may damage the land, causing **erosion**.

Desert landscapes

The appearance of deserts varies a great deal. High mountains, shifting sand dunes, vast expanses of stony ground, and huge boulders are all found in different deserts throughout the world. Some deserts have all these different types of landscape. Death Valley in the United States has dry lake beds covered in layers of glistening salt, called **saltpans**. But in Antarctica, large areas are completely covered in thick sheets of ice.

▼ Sometimes, all the sand is blown away from a desert area, leaving bare rocks.

▲ Floodwaters flowing into a desert valley may become trapped and form a lake. As the lake dries out, it leaves a layer of salt. The layers of salt build up until the whole area becomes a saltpan.

▶ Some of the rock formations in the Great Basin, in the western United States rise as high as 990 feet (300 m). The landscape there has been worn away over thousands of years, creating columns of rock called **buttes**, and shaping the stronger rocks into flat-topped hills known as **mesas**.

DISK LINK
Could you survive in a barren desert? Put yourself to the test in DESERTED!

Hot deserts

The world's largest hot desert is called the Sahara. It stretches across northern Africa, from the Atlantic Ocean in the west, to the Red Sea in the east. Altogether, the Sahara covers about 3½ million square miles (9 million sq. km), which is about the size of the United States.

More than 10,000 years ago, the climate of the Sahara was much wetter than it is today, and the region was covered with vegetation. But about 6,000 years ago, the climate began to change, gradually becoming much drier and turning the Sahara into a desert.

▲ Sand dunes form as grains of sand pile up against rocks or other obstacles.

Oases

An **oasis** is a **fertile** area where underground water flows to the surface, or where there is a permanent river. There are about 90 large oases in the Sahara. People live and grow crops in these areas.

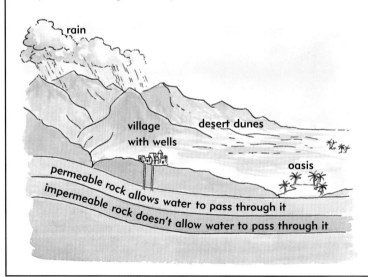

rain

village with wells

desert dunes

oasis

permeable rock allows water to pass through it

impermeable rock doesn't allow water to pass through it

The Sahara is one of the hottest areas in the world. The highest temperature in the world—136 °F (58 °C)—was recorded here. On average, the Sahara receives less than 4 inches (10 cm) of rain each year, and some areas receive as little as 1 inch (2.5 cm).

The landscape of the Sahara varies. In the center, the Ahaggar Mountains rise steeply. In the northeast, there is a region of rocky **plateaus** known as the Tassil-n-Ajjer. Much of the Sahara is sandy. In the north and west of the Sahara, there are vast seas of sand called **ergs**. On the edges of the Sahara there are dry grasslands where few trees grow.

▼ This is an oasis. Such a fertile area is an unusual sight in a desert landscape.

DID YOU KNOW?

● Sand is actually tiny pieces of rock and **minerals** that form when larger rocks crumble away.

● Sand dunes move with the wind. Sometimes, strong winds can move a dune by up to 12 inches (30 cm) in a day. This may mean that a settlement on the edge of a desert is gradually covered with sand, forcing the people who live there to move to another area.

● In the Sahara, some of the sand dunes are 600 feet (180 m) high!

● Desert travelers sometimes see a trick of light known as a **mirage**. They think that they can see a pool of water in the distance. But when they reach the spot, they find only dry sand. A mirage is created when a ray of light bends as it passes first through cold air and then through warm air.

Cold deserts

Some of the coldest places in the world are dry deserts. The air in these areas is too cold to release moisture, so they receive very little rain.

Antarctica is the coldest place in the world. In 1983, the temperature there dropped to 120 °F (-89 °C). Most of the time, the temperature there doesn't rise above 32 °F (0 °C). This icy continent at the South Pole is also one of the world's driest deserts. Some parts of Antarctica don't receive any rain at all, while other parts receive less than 2 inches (5 cm) of moisture every year, usually in the form of snow and ice crystals.

Few plants and animals can survive in Antarctica. However, tiny living things known as algae grow on the ice and snow. Some animals and birds, such as seals and penguins, live on the coast. The only people living in Antarctica are the 1,000 scientists who work on scientific stations here.

The Arctic, on the other hand, is home to many groups of native people. During summer in some places around the North Pole, the temperature may reach 61 °F (16 °C). This is warm enough to melt the snow and ice. Plants burst into life, and many animals and birds visit to feed on the new vegetation.

The lands of both the polar regions are rich in natural minerals. In the Arctic, people mine gold, oil, copper, and tin. In Antarctica, however, mining is forbidden because it could destroy this unique environment.

▼ Emperor penguins in Antarctica

DISK LINK
You'll have a chance to explore the world's coldest deserts when you play **WHERE IN THE WORLD?**

Desert animals

Animals that live in hot deserts have adapted to the warm, dry climate. The main problem for desert animals is the lack of water. Some animals have ways of storing water in their bodies. Others get all the moisture they need from the plants and insects they eat.

▼ Camels can travel for days without having to eat or drink. The fat contained in a camel's hump acts like a food supply and provides the animal with the energy it needs to survive.

▶ This is a sidewinder snake with its head buried in the sand. These snakes move sideways across the sand, keeping most of their body above the ground.

◀ The gila monster is a type of lizard found in the deserts of the southwestern United States and northern Mexico. It has a **venomous** bite to kill prey. The gila monster stores fat in its tail and can go for months without food.

DISK LINK
Get to know some desert animals and find out what they're having for dinner when you play DINNER TIME.

Many desert animals move around at night, when it is cooler. During the day, they find shelter under rocks and plants or in underground burrows. Animals that move around in the daytime heat often have ways of avoiding the hot sand. For example, kangaroo rats in the deserts of the southwestern United States have long back legs to hop quickly over the ground.

Creatures such as snakes and lizards, which are cold-blooded, need to warm themselves in the heat of the sun before they can move around. They hide in the shade when the sun is at its hottest.

Fennec
The fennec, a fox of the Sahara, has large ears that help it to release heat from its body and stay cool.

Desert plants

In order to survive in the harsh desert conditions, desert plants must make use of every drop of water. Plants lose a lot of water through their leaves, so in dry deserts many plants have tiny leaves that allow only a small amount of water to escape. Other plants shed their leaves during long periods when there is no rain.

Some desert plants have long, tough roots that reach deep underground in search of moisture. The roots of the mesquite bush in the deserts of the United States stretch 40 feet (12 m) below the ground! Many cactuses have roots that spread over a wide area just below the surface. Water is carried up through the roots and stored in the stem of the plant.

A number of plants do not grow at all during periods of **drought**. They lie as seeds in the soil, waiting for rain. When at last rain falls, the seeds sprout quickly in the damp earth and, within days, the desert is covered in plants and flowers.

▼ These flowers in the Kalahari Desert have burst into life after a rare period of rain. They will bloom for only a few days until the desert dries out again.

DID YOU KNOW?

● Some types of cacti can live for up to 200 years.

● The leaves of the desert holly plant grow almost vertically, or straight up. This means that the hot sunlight catches only the edges of the leaves, so they don't lose a lot of their moisture.

● A type of cactus called the jumping cholla has stems that fall off so easily that they seem to jump on people or animals passing by!

▶ The giant saguaro cactus is found in the deserts of the southwestern United States and northwestern Mexico. After rain has fallen, the saguaro's waxy stems swell as they fill up with water and the cactus lives on this water until the next rainfall. As much as 80 per cent of a saguaro is made up of water. Some giant saguaros grow to a height of 60 feet (18 m).

DISK LINK
See if you've got what it takes to make the desert bloom in **BREAK THE DROUGHT.**

Changing shapes

Although very little rain falls in desert areas, much of the shaping of the desert landscape is caused by water. When rain does fall, it is very heavy. The hard, dry soil cannot soak up the all water, so it runs down the slopes, causing flash floods. The water carves out steep-sided valleys known as **wadis**. Rocks, boulders, and pebbles are carried down from the valleys to the desert plain.

▶ This round boulder was shaped by water and the wind.

The wind also helps to shape desert areas. Sand dunes are created by wind. Sometimes the sand and soil are blown away completely, leaving bare rock surfaces known as rock pavements. Fierce winds can blow the sand with great force and cause erosion.

Rocks on the surface of a desert are affected by temperature, too. During the day they are heated. Then at night, the rocks cool down. The constant heating and cooling weakens the rocks until eventually they crack.

◀ These eroded sandstone columns are in the Tassili-n-Ajjer plateaus of the Sahara.

◀ These rock formations are called badlands. They were created by the movements of wind and water. The stripes show how the sand was moved before it dried into hard layers of rock. The badlands in this picture are in the Great Basin of the western United States.

Wadis

A wadi is is created when water rushes over a dry desert slope.

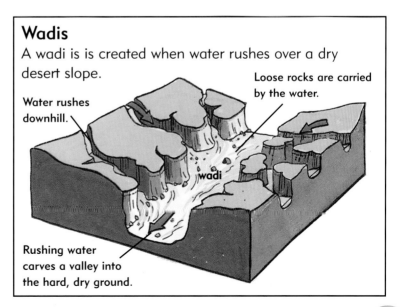

Loose rocks are carried by the water.

Water rushes downhill.

wadi

Rushing water carves a valley into the hard, dry ground.

Survival skills

Traditionally, many groups of desert people, such as the Bedouins of Arabia, were **nomads**. Instead of living in permanent homes, they moved from place to place, putting up temporary shelters wherever they stopped. Their animals provided meat and milk, as well as wool and skins used to make clothing and tents. They traded with other desert people, exchanging goods such as wool, leather, rice, and grain.

Although some nomadic tribes still follow the traditional way of life, many have abandoned it. Now, most desert people spend only part of each year traveling, while others live in permanent campsites or villages near oases.

One reason for this changing way of life is that many desert people wish to move to towns and cities in search of work. Another reason is that some governments have made it difficult for people to travel between countries. Severe droughts have also made it harder for nomadic people to survive.

DISK LINK
Find out more about the traditional way of life of desert people in the TREK TO TIMBUKTU.

▼ This Bedouin is taking care of a herd of sheep and goats.

Make a solar still

Building a solar still is a way of collecting water from the ground. Desert travelers often build solar stills to catch water. In hot weather, try making a still of your own on a beach or in the yard.

You will need:
● a spade
● a jar or tin can
● a sheet of plastic wrap
● stones

1. Dig a hole about 3 feet (1 m) across and 12 inches (60 cm) deep and place the jar or tin can in the center of it.

2. Spread the plastic wrap over the hole and secure the edges with stones.

3. Place a stone on the plastic wrap directly above the jar or tin can. The sun will heat the soil beneath the plastic wrap. Moisture will then form on the plastic wrap and drip down into the jar or can. So all you have to do now is wait for the water to collect! **Warning:** Don't drink the water! It isn't clean enough to drink!

Science at work

It is difficult to grow crops in dry desert lands. Scientists have developed many ways of watering the ground in some deserts to make them fertile. People can build a network of canals to carry water from a lake or river to their farmlands. Or, where water lies deep underground, people can dig wells to pump water to the surface. Watering the land in this way is called **irrigation**.

Many desert lands contain valuable minerals. Diamonds are mined in the Namib Desert in southwestern Africa, and there are huge copper and **sodium nitrate** mines in the Atacama Desert in South America. Gold, uranium, and aluminum have been discovered in the Australian Desert, and there is oil and natural gas in parts of the Great Basin, Sahara, and Arabian deserts.

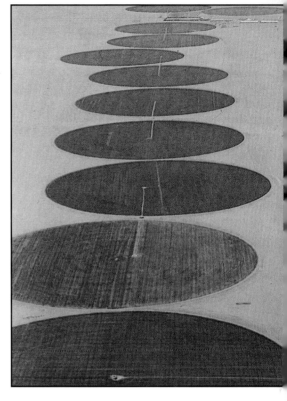

▲ These circular wheat fields in Libya are watered by pipes that move like the hands of a clock. The water is pumped from deep under the ground.

◄ Narrow ditches called furrows can be dug to carry water between rows of crops. The water flows into the furrows through pipes with holes in them.

Some deserts receive lots of sunlight that can be collected and turned into electricity. This method of making electricity is called **solar power**. One way to make solar power is to lay many mirrors out over an area of land. The mirrors focus the sun's rays onto a target. Then a special fluid is heated as it passes through pipes under the target. The hot fluid makes steam or gas that is pumped to a nearby power station. The heat energy in the steam or gas powers turbines to generate electricity.

▲ This is an open-pit copper mine in the Great Basin.

DISK LINK
Want to know more about desertification? Then ask the expert in KEEPING COOL.

DISK LINK
Want to know more about desertification? Then ask the expert in KEEPING COOL.

DID YOU KNOW?

● Each year, many of the world's deserts grow bigger. This is partly because of Earth's changing climate, but the main reason is human activity. Grazing cattle and livestock strip the ground of its vegetation and make fertile land around the edges of some deserts barren. Huge mining and lumbering projects also increase the size of some deserts. This process is called desertification.

The search for the lost city

As soon as Harry Philby heard the name Wabar, he decided that he would be the person to find this legendary lost city. For many years, storytellers had talked of the capital of King 'Ad Ibn Kin'ad, which lay deep in the Rub' al Khali Desert in Arabia. Here, according to legend, there were palaces encrusted in gems and surrounded by gardens of exotic flowers. But one awful day, the entire city was destroyed by fire.

By the time Harry Philby heard the stories of Wabar, the city had been lost for more than 7,000 years. It was said to have existed on the banks of a river that had long since been covered over by the shifting desert sands. The desert in this region was known to the local people as The Empty Quarter.

The people warned of the terrible dangers that lay within the desert. The sands, they said, were littered with

But Philby was determined. He set out on January 6, 1932, with 18 men and 32 camels loaded with supplies. On the first night, as Philby stood by the campfire talking, he fainted. His face turned yellow, and his companions were convinced that he was going to die. They wrapped him up warmly and took turns sitting by him until morning. When he awoke, he felt perfectly well. The mystery illness had passed.

The expedition moved on. But their journey seemed to be cursed with bad luck. First the weather turned so bitterly cold that the drinking water froze. Then, a few days later it became unbearably hot. Grains of sand were whipped up all around the men, turning their faces raw. Still, the camels trudged on through the sand.

the bleached skeletons of travelers and their camels who had perished in the burning heat there.

It wasn't long before the water ran out. The men urgently searched for wells buried deep in the sand. They were fortunate enough to find a well. But they had to spend hours digging before they reached the water, which was deep underground.

The party continued, crossing the beds of two ancient, dried-up rivers. After several days, they came to a third riverbed. This was, Philby believed, the river on which the legendary city of Wabar had stood. That night, they camped within only a day's journey of Wabar. Philby tossed and turned on his camp bed that night, dreaming of reaching the long-lost city.

The next day the party marched on, following the river's course.

"Look!" shouted one of the men.

Philby shaded his eyes against the sun. On the crest of a distant ridge, he saw what appeared to be a low line of ruins.

Philby urged his camel on, thrilled by the idea of turning his dream into reality. When he reached the top of the ridge, he jumped down from his camel and ran across the sand.

But then Philby sank to his knees with a groan. He was looking down on the remains of an old volcano! Most of the volcano had been filled with sand, but its rocky edge could still be seen.

Philby was overwhelmed with disappointment. He realized that the legendary city of Wabar still lay hidden somewhere deep beneath the shifting desert sands.

The next day the men demanded to leave the area. But Philby did not want the trip to be wasted. Instead of heading back the way they had come, Philby ordered his weary companions to travel across 1,980 miles (600 km) of hot, waterless desert. The exhausted men pressed their thirsty camels on through the drought-stricken land. None of the men, who had lived in the desert all their lives, had ever seen such a desolate place! But finally, on March 14, over two months since the journey began, they emerged from the desert—the first people in history to cross the Empty Quarter from side to side.

Desert fact-file

Photocopy this page and use the chart to jot down your findings as you explore the disk. All of the facts and figures you need to complete the chart can be found in WHERE IN THE WORLD?

Name of desert	Annual rainfall	Highest temperature	Lowest temperature
Antarctica			
Arabian Desert			
Arctic			
Atacama Desert			
Australian Desert			
Great Basin			
Gobi Desert			
Kalahari Desert			
Karakum			
Kyzyl Kum			
Namib Desert			
Patagonian Desert			
Sahara			
Taklimakan Desert			
Thar Desert			

True or false?

Which of these facts are true and which are false?
If you have read the book carefully, you will know the answers!

1. Sand consists of tiny pieces of rocks and minerals.

2. All deserts are hot.

3. Most desert animals move about during the day.

4. The Sahara used to be covered with vegetation.

5. Mesas and buttes are types of cacti.

6. Oases are fertile areas in the desert.

7. Sand covers half of all desert areas.

8. A mirage is a trick of light.

9. The temperature in a hot desert falls at night.

10. Coastal deserts are always separated from the sea by mountains.

11. Many desert peoples no longer follow a nomadic way of life.

12. Some desert plants store water in their stems.

ANSWERS: 1.T 2.F 3.F 4.T 5.F 6.T 7.F 8.T 9.T 10.F 11.T 12.T

Desert word search

Photocopy this page and see if you can solve this desert word puzzle.
All of the words listed below can be found either forward, backward, or diagonally.

F	E	R	T	I	L	E	W	E	B	N	P
L	S	A	L	T	P	A	N	S	U	V	L
A	L	D	R	Y	D	R	E	R	T	N	A
S	A	R	A	I	N	N	S	E	T	O	T
H	R	O	S	I	U	A	N	W	E	I	E
F	E	U	U	D	S	O	S	O	S	T	A
L	N	G	O	E	I	A	O	P	D	A	U
O	I	H	M	S	N	S	H	R	A	G	S
O	M	T	O	E	G	E	O	A	M	I	D
D	M	R	N	R	N	S	T	L	O	R	N
V	E	G	E	T	A	T	I	O	N	R	A
S	U	N	V	D	L	O	C	S	T	I	S

buttes	dunes	flash flood	minerals	rain	sun
cold	ergs	hot	nomads	saltpan	vegetation
drought	erosion	irrigation	oases	sand	venomous
dry	fertile	mesas	plateaus	solar power	wadis

Glossary

Buttes
Columns of rock in desert areas that have been worn away by wind, water, and heat.

Drought
A long period of dry weather, with no rainfall at all.

Environment
A word used to describe the climate and landscape, as well as the human, animal, and plant life, of a region.

Ergs
Huge areas of moving sand.

Erosion
The wearing away of parts of the earth's surface by wind, water, and heat.

Fertile
Soil is fertile when it contains enough water and minerals for plants to grow.

Flash floods
Sudden, violent floods that occur when heavy rain falls in a desert. If the ground is hard and dry, the water rushes over the surface instead of soaking in. The force of the water wears away the land.

Irrigation
Methods of supplying water to dry areas. Building canals or digging wells, in order to make the land suitable for growing crops, are examples of irrigation.

Mesas
Large, flat-topped hills formed by erosion over thousands of years.

Minerals
Natural, nonliving substances, such as salt or tin, that are found in the ground.

Mirage
An optical illusion caused by heat. In the desert, a mirage may cause people to believe they see a pool of water in the distance.

Nomads
People who have no permanent home but travel from place to place, building temporary shelters wherever they stop.

Oasis
A fertile area in a desert, where underground water flows to the surface or where there is a permanent river.

Plateaus
Areas of high, flat land.

Saltpan
A layer of salt on a dry lake bed.

Sodium nitrate
A type of mineral used to make matches, explosives, and fertilizers.

Solar power
Energy from the sun that is used to make electricity.

Vegetation
The plant life of an area.

Venomous
A word to describe an animal that uses poison to kill its prey.

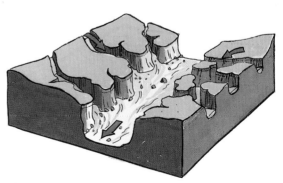

Wadis
Steep-sided valleys in desert areas that have been carved out by water.

Loading your INTERFACT disk

INTERFACT is easy to load.
But before you begin,
quickly run through
the checklist on the
next page to
ensure that your
computer is ready
to run the program.

Your INTERFACT
CD-ROM will run on
both PCs with Windows
and on Macintoshes. To make
sure that your computer meets
the system requirements, check the list below.

SYSTEM REQUIREMENTS

PC
- 486DX2/66 MHz Processor
- Windows 3.1, 3.11, 95, 98 (or later)
- 8 MB RAM (16 MB recommended for Windows 95 and 24 MB recommended for Windows 98)
- VGA color monitor
- Soundblaster-compatible sound card

MACINTOSH
- 68020 processor
- system 7.0 (or later)
- 16 MB of RAM

LOADING INSTRUCTIONS

You can run INTERFACT from the disk – you don't need to install it on your hard drive.

PC WITH WINDOWS 95 OR 98

The program should start automatically when you put the disk in the CD drive. If it does not, follow these instructions.

1. Put the disk in the CD drive
2. Open MY COMPUTER
3. Double-click on the CD drive icon
4. Double-click on the icon called DESERTS 95

PC WITH WINDOWS 3.1 OR 3.11

1. Put the disk in the CD drive
2. Select RUN from the FILE menu in the PROGRAM MANAGER
3. Type D:\DESERTS (where D is the letter of your CD drive)
4. Press the RETURN key

MACINTOSH

1. Put the disk in the CD drive
2. Double click on the INTERFACT icon
3. Double click on the icon called DESERTS

CHECKLIST

- First make sure that your computer and monitor meet the system requirements as described on page 38.

- Ensure that your computer, monitor, and CD-ROM drive are all turned on and working normally.

- It is important that no other applications, such as word processors, are running. Before starting INTERFACT quit all other applications.

- Make sure that the screen saver has been turned off.

- If you are running INTERFACT on a PC with Windows 3.1 or 3.11, make sure that you type in the correct instructions when loading the disk, using a colon (:), not a semi-colon (;) and a back slash (\), not a forward slash (/). Also, do not use any other punctuation or put any spaces between letters.

How to use INTERFACT

INTERFACT is easy to use.
First see page 38 to find out how to
load the program. Then read
these simple instructions and dive in!

There are seven different features to explore. Use the controls on the right-hand side of the screen to select the one you want to play. You will see that the main area of the screen changes as you click on different features.

For example, this is what your screen will look like when you play KEEPING COOL, where Leo the Lizard will answer all your questions. Once you've selected a feature, click on the main screen to start playing.

Why are some deserts cold?

Click on Leo for the answer.

Click here to select the feature you want to play.

Click on the arrow keys to scroll through the different features on the disk or to find your way to the exit.

Click here to hear the text read or to turn the sound off.

This is the text box, where instructions and directions appear. Go to page 4 to find out what's on the disk.

DISK LINKS

When you read the book, you'll come across Disk Links. These show you where to find activities on the disk that relate to the page you are reading. Use the arrow keys to find the icon on screen that matches the one in the Disk Link.

DISK LINK
You can visit all the world's major deserts when you play WHERE IN THE WORLD?

BOOKMARKS

As you explore the features on the disk, you'll bump into Bookmarks. These show you where to look in the book for more information about the topic on screen. Just turn to the page of the book shown in the Bookmark.

23

ACTIVITIES

On pages 33-35, there are some fun activities for you to complete. Photocopy these pages and use them as you go through the book and the disk.

HOT DISK TIPS

● If you don't know how to use one of the on-screen controls, simply touch it with your cursor. An explanation will pop up in the text box.

● Any words that appear on screen in a different color and underlined are "hot." This means that you can touch them with the cursor for more information.

● Keep a close eye on the cursor. When it changes from an arrow ➔ to a hand, ☞ click your mouse and something will happen.

● In some of the features, your cursor will change into a special tool, such as a magnifying glass ⊶⊕ or a thermometer. ⊏▭ When this happens, click on that part of the screen to learn more about what's happening there.

Troubleshooting

 If you come across a problem loading or running the INTERFACT disk, you should find the solution here. If you still cannot solve your problem, call the helpline at 1-609-921-6700

COMMON PROBLEMS

 Cannot load disk
There is not enough space available on your hard disk. To make more space available, delete old applications and programs you don't use until 6 MB of free space is available.

 There is no sound (PCs only)
Your sound card is not Soundblaster compatible. To make your settings Soundblaster compatible, see your sound card manual for more information.

 Disk will not run
There is not enough memory available. Quit all other applications and programs. If this does not work, increase your machine's RAM by adjusting the Virtual Memory (see right).

 There is no sound
Your speakers or headphones are not connected to the CD-ROM drive. Ensure that your speakers or headphones are connected to the speaker outlet at the back of your computer.

 Print-outs are not centered on the page or are partly cut off
Make sure that the page layout is set to "Landscape" in the Print dialog box.

 There is no sound
Ensure that the volume control is turned up (on your external speakers and by using internal volume control).

Graphics freeze or text boxes appear blank (Windows 95 or 98 only)

The graphics card acceleration is too high. To fix this, right-click on MY COMPUTER. Then, click on PROPERTIES, then PERFORMANCE, then GRAPHICS. Reset the hardware acceleration slider to "None." Click OK. After doing this, you will need to restart your computer.

Text does not fit into boxes or hot words do not work

The standard fonts on your computer have been moved or deleted. You will need to the reinstall the standard fonts for your computer. PC users require Arial. Macintosh users require Helvetica. Please see your computer manual for further information.

Your machine freezes

There is not enough memory available. Either quit other applications and programs or increase your machine's RAM by adjusting the Virtual Memory (see right).

Graphics do not load or are of poor quality

Not enough memory is available, or you have the wrong display setting. Either quit other applications and programs or make sure that your monitor control is set to 256 colors (MAC) or VGA (PC).

HOW TO...

Reset screen resolution in Windows 3.1 or 3.11:

In Program Manager, double-click on MAIN. Double-click on OPTIONS, then click on "Change system settings." Reset the screen resolution to 640 x 480, 256 colors. You will need to restart your computer after changing display settings.

Reset screen resolution in Windows 95 or 98:

Click on START at the bottom left of your screen, then click on SETTINGS, then CONTROL PANEL, then double-click on DISPLAY. Click on the SETTINGS tab at the top. Reset the Desktop area (or Display area) to 640 x 480 pixels, then click APPLY. You may need to restart your computer after changing display settings.

Reset screen resolution for Macintosh:

Click on the Apple symbol at the top left of your screen to access APPLE MENU ITEMS. Select CONTROL PANELS, then MONITORS (or MONITORS AND SOUND), then set the resolution to 640 x 480.

Adjust the Virtual Memory in Windows 95 or 98:

Open MY COMPUTER, then click on CONTROL PANEL, then SYSTEMS. Select PERFORMANCE, click on VIRTUAL MEMORY, and set the preferred size to a higher value.

Adjust the Virtual Memory on Apple Macintosh:

If you have 16 MB of RAM or more, DESERTS will run faster. Select the DESERTS icon and go to GET INFO in the FILE folder. Set the preferred (or current) size to a higher value.

Index

CD (PC/MAC) ISBN 1-58728-451-0

CD (PC/MAC) ISBN 1-58728-460-X

CD (PC/MAC) ISBN 1-58728-463-4

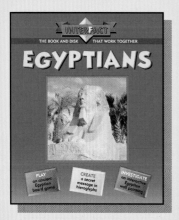

CD (PC/MAC) ISBN 1-58728-458-8

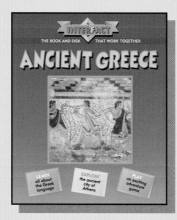

CD (PC/MAC) ISBN 1-58728-455-3

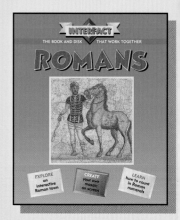

CD (PC/MAC) ISBN 1-58728-462-6

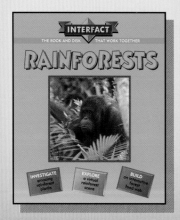

CD (PC/MAC) ISBN 1-58728-461-8

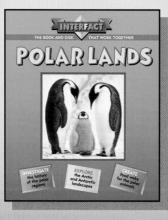

CD (PC/MAC) ISBN 1-58728-452-9

CD (PC/MAC) ISBN 1-58728-459-6

WATCH FOR NEW TITLES!

CD (PC/MAC) ISBN 1-58728-470-7

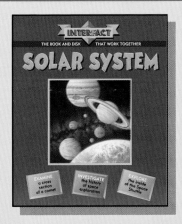

CD (PC/MAC) ISBN 1-58728-464-2

CD (PC/MAC) ISBN 1-58728-465-0

CD (PC/MAC) ISBN 1-58728-450-2

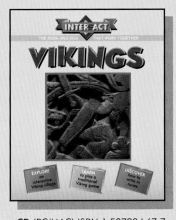

CD (PC/MAC) ISBN 1-58728-467-7

There is a wide array of INTERFACT titles to choose from, covering science, history, and nature.

And if you turn the page, you'll discover the new INTERFACT REFERENCE series of books and disk.

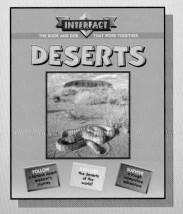

CD (PC/MAC) ISBN 1-58728-457-X

CD (PC/MAC) ISBN 1-58728-468-5

Look for the new INTERFACT REFERENCE series.
Each large, colorful book works with an exciting disk, opening up
whole new areas of learning and providing a great reference source.

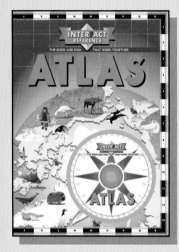

CD (PC/MAC) ISBN 1-58728-471-5   CD (PC/MAC) ISBN 1-58728-473-1   CD (PC/MAC) ISBN 1-58728-472-3

INTERFACT REFERENCE

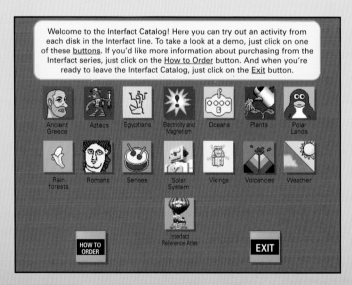

Welcome to the Interact Catalog! Here you can try out an activity from each disk in the Interact line. To take a look at a demo, just click on one of these buttons. If you'd like more information about purchasing from the Interact series, just click on the How to Order button. And when you're ready to leave the Interact Catalog, just click on the Exit button.

Ancient Greece · Aztecs · Egyptians · Electricity and Magnetism · Oceans · Plants · Polar Lands · Rain forests · Romans · Senses · Solar System · Vikings · Volcanoes · Weather · Interact Reference Atlas

HOW TO ORDER

EXIT

Make sure that you check out the INTERFACT Catalog on your INTERFACT CD-ROM.

You'll find a feature to play from each of the titles in the INTERFACT series.

For all orders or more information on other Two-Can books and multimedia contact.
Two-Can Publishing LLC, 234 Nassau Street, Princeton, NJ 08542
Call 1-609-921-6700, fax 1-609-921-3349 or visit our web site at
http://www.two-canpublishing.com